Katy Duck
Goes to Work

By Alyssa Satin Capucilli   Illustrated by Henry Cole

Ready-to-Read

Simon Spotlight

New York   London   Toronto   Sydney   New Delhi

For all the wonderful moms and dads who
bring their children to work . . . including my own!
—A. S. C.

SIMON SPOTLIGHT
An imprint of Simon & Schuster Children's Publishing Division
1230 Avenue of the Americas, New York, New York 10020
Text copyright © 2014 by Alyssa Satin Capucilli
Illustrations copyright © 2014 by Henry Cole
For information about special discounts for bulk purchases, please contact Simon & Schuster
Special Sales at 1-866-506-1949 or business@simonandschuster.com.
The Simon & Schuster Speakers Bureau can bring authors to your live event. For more information or
to book an event contact the Simon & Schuster Speakers Bureau at 1-866-248-3049 or visit our website
at www.simonspeakers.com.
Manufactured in the United States of America 0314 LAK
First Edition
10 9 8 7 6 5 4 3 2 1
Library of Congress Cataloging-in-Publication Data
Capucilli, Alyssa Satin, 1957-
Katy Duck goes to work / by Alyssa Satin Capucilli ; illustrated by Henry
Cole. — First edition.
pages cm. — (Ready-to-read)
Summary: Katy is excited to spend a day with her father at work and
enjoys typing, pressing buttons, visiting the watercooler, and coloring but
quickly learns to be careful when dancing at work.
ISBN 978-1-4424-7281-5 (pbk) — ISBN 978-1-4424-7282-2 (hc) —
ISBN 978-1-4424-7283-9 (ebook) [1. Fathers and daughters—Fiction.
2. Work—Fiction. 3. Offices—Fiction. 4. Ducks—Fiction.] I. Cole, Henry,
illustrator. II. Title.
PZ7.C179Kh 2014
[E]—dc23
2013012967

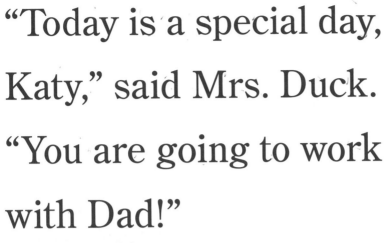

"Today is a special day, Katy," said Mrs. Duck. "You are going to work with Dad!"

"Tra-la-la. Quack! Quack!"
Katy was so excited.
She had never gone to
work before.

Katy chose her best tutu.
She put on her boa and
a sparkly crown.

Then Katy danced
into the living room.
Katy Duck loved to dance.

"Tra-la-la. Quack! Quack!
I am ready for work!"
she said.

Katy leaped and spun
all the way to the
bus stop.

She looked out
the bus window.
The trees swayed
like ballerinas!

It was a busy day at work for Katy Duck.

Katy typed

She pressed lots of buttons.

She visited the watercooler.

She colored with crayons.

"Tra-la-la. Quack! Quack! Work is fun," said Katy. "But not as much fun as dancing!"

Katy whirled.

She pranced.

She twirled.

"Tra-la-la. Quack! Quack!"
Katy danced here.

Katy danced there.

"Tra-la-la—"

BUMP! THUMP!

Katy sent papers flying

everywhere!

"Oh no, Katy,"
said Mr. Duck.
He looked upset.

Very upset.

Katy looked right.

Katy looked left.

Katy looked down.

"Now, now, Katy,"
said Mr. Duck.

"I know you love to dance. But at work, you must dance a bit more carefully. Okay?"

Katy nodded.

She helped Mr. Duck

clean up the papers.

Then she helped Mr. Duck
order lunch.
They even shared an
ice-cream sundae!

"Tra-la-la. Quack! Quack!
How I love ice cream,"
said Katy Duck.

"Tra-la-la. Quack! Quack! And how I love going to work with you," she said.

Mr. Duck smiled and
gave Katy a spin.
"Tra-la-la. Wheee!"
They danced all the way
home.